For Lewis, Joshua and Georgia.

Published in association with Bear With Us Productions

ISBN: 978-1-7392320-1-6

Illustration by Andri Anto
Graphic design by Katie Owens

www.justbearwithus.com

Written by Tim Fenton

Illustrated By Andri Anto

This is the story
Of Doogle McFrugal
Who lives in a village
Called Invershoogle.

It's a funny old place
That's hard to discover,
Surrounded by forests
And mountains for cover.

There are no roads for driving.
The weather is shocking.
The only way in is by pony
Or walking.

Doogle's wee house is
Creaking and cracking,
The roof's full of holes
With an old chimney stack in.

The windows are boarded,
The door hanging squinty,
Waiting for fixing
By Hamish McGinty

A three-legged table,
Chairs with no stuffing.
All the time Doogle
Is huffing and puffing.

He has a smelly old cat,
A dog and a parrot
With a bright orange beak
Shaped just like a carrot.

His garden is planted
With tatties and neeps.
He gets eggs for boiling
From a hen that he keeps.

Fish from the river,
Fruit from the trees,
Haggis in season,
And honey from bees.

He doesn't need much
To get by day to day.
No shops to go spending,
No bills to pay.

No TV for watching,
No radio or phone,
No neighbours for miles,
He's all on his own.

But, for thirty-five years,
Each morning from nine,
He works all day
Way down in a mine.

Scratching and scraping,

Digging and poking.

It's cold and damp

And Doogle gets soaking.

Nothing to show

For his hard work and toil,

But blisters and bruises

And covered in soil.

And still every morning,
Come hail, rain or snow,
There's only one place
For Doogle to go.

A mile underground,
Lit by a lamp,
In the deep, dark mine,
He works in the damp.

One day, while out working,
After he dug it,
He looks at the mine wall
And there is a nugget!

He puts on his glasses,
So his eyes can behold
A huge lump of metal,
Unmistakably... Gold!

He screams and he hollers,
Runs as fast as is able
To the creaky old house
And the three-legged table.

Doogle uncovers
His new golden treasure,
The thing that could change
His whole life forever.

He's dreamed of this moment
For years and years.
Old Doogle's eyes
Are filling with tears.

"I'll fix up the roof,
And the squinty old door.
A leg for the table
And so much more!"

"I'll need a computer,
A large screen TV,
Kitchen extension,
A bed and settee!"

"A plough and a tractor.
I'll build a huge barn,
And a big double garage
To keep my new car in!"

"I'll be rich and famous
And give interviews,
Get chased by photographers,
Be in the news!"

"The world will know me —
I'm Doogle McFrugal!
They'll all come and visit
To Invershoogle...!"

"A gold rush will start,
Huge diggers arrive,
Tearing up trees,
Building roads and a drive."

"Motorways, airports,
A railroad or three.
It'll all be my fault,
And all down to me."

"The place will go crazy,
They'll all be manic!"

Suddenly Doogle

Is caught in a panic.

"I can't let this happen!"

He runs down the mine,

Puts back the nugget,

And covers in slime.

Fills in the entrance

With mud, rocks and rubble.

He decides that the gold mine

Is far too much trouble.

He fixes his roof.

The windows are gleaming.

Doogle is happy,

A big smile is beaming.

No more cracking or creaking,

The front door is straight,

A four-legged table with

Soft chairs await.

He shampoos the cat,

The dog gets fed.

The parrot keeps talking

Till they all go to bed.

"I'm ever so happy!

I'm no longer sad!

All that I needed...

I already had!"

Printed in Great Britain
by Amazon